Praise for
Kristine Kathryn Rusch

"Rusch is a great storyteller."
—*RT Book Reviews*

"Whether [Rusch] writes high fantasy, horror, sf, or contemporary fantasy, I've always been fascinated by her ability to tell a story with that enviable gift of invisible prose. She's one of those very few writers whose style takes me right into the story—the words and pages disappear as the characters and their story swallows me whole…. Rusch has style."
—Charles de Lint

"Kristine Kathryn Rusch is one of the best writers in the field and 'Dragon's Tooth' does not disappoint…Rusch gives us a delightful tale here!."
—*SFRevu*

"…the always impressive Rusch can successfully tackle any genre she sets her sights on."
—Barnes & Noble.com

Also by
Kristine Kathryn Rusch

THE ABRACABRA INCORPORATED SERIES

The Assassin's Dagger (short story)
Dragon's Tooth

THE FAERIE JUSTICE SERIES

Show Trial
The War and After (short-story collection)

THE FEY SERIES

Destiny
The Sacrifice
The Changeling
The Rival
The Resistance
Victory
The Black Queen
The Black King

Dragon's Tooth

AN ABRACADABRA INCORPORATED NOVELLA

KRISTINE KATHRYN RUSCH

*wmg*PUBLISHING

Dragon's Tooth

Published 2013 by WMG Publishing
www.wmgpublishing.com
First published in *Baen's Universe*, August, 2008
Cover art copyright © Sanja Baljkas/Dreamstime
Book and cover design copyright © 2013 by WMG Publishing
Cover design by Allyson Longueira/WMG Publishing
ISBN-13: 978-0-615-88637-4
ISBN-10: 0-615-88637-X

Dragon's Tooth

AN ABRACADABRA INCORPORATED NOVELLA

1

THE LAST PLACE Tara expected to find magical items was in a tourist shop on the rue de Rivoli. The shop was tiny, perhaps twenty-five square feet, with glass shelves recessed into the wall and a one-person counter made of brick. Most of the touristy merchandise—the usual postcards, canvas bags with pictures of the Eiffel Tower, and Toulouse-Latrec mugs—were on rack displays on the sidewalk outside.

Inside, though, she found a treasure trove. Mingled among the delicate Limoges china and the petite Lalique glass sculptures were unique items: cloisonné that looked authentically medieval, perfume bottles made from glass so old it was cloudy, and little crosses that appeared to be made of hammered, stamped gold.

She was the only customer inside, but outside tourists gathered around the postcards, discussing the choices in loud voices. A few of the tourists spoke English; the rest were speaking Japanese or German.

It was her personal curse that she understood banal conversation in all three languages.

Horns honked and someone shouted an expletive in French. She made herself focus on the items on the backlit shelf before her, trying not to feel overwhelmed.

It had been eight months since she had been to Paris. Eight quiet months in which she revamped the store she'd taken over in the Loire Valley. It had taken two months to cleanse the stench of the dark arts from the place, and two more to find the right merchandise. Then she had to suffer the ridicule of the locals who did not believe an American—no matter what her experience—should run a magic shop that had been in their fair city for hundreds of years.

She wasn't making a profit yet. She doubted that would happen for another two years or more. But she was finally making enough to hire an assistant, and the assistant's presence enabled her to come to Paris on a buying trip.

And to get away.

Most of the items on the backlit shelf were small— ruby-encrusted thimbles and china tea cups so tiny that no doll could hold them. But in the middle of the shelf, someone had laid a fringed bit of tapestry. Its ragged edges suggested that it had been torn off a larger piece.

Above the tapestry, someone had taped a small sign. In black India ink, someone had calligraphed a single word. Relique. Relic, in English. Or, more properly, relics.

Bits and pieces of a past that probably had not existed: a splinter of wood from the True Cross; shards from a Roman burial urn; and a lock of dusty-looking hair shaped like a broach, purported to be taken from St. Peter's body shortly after he died.

Next to the hair was a long bone-colored piece in the shape of a dagger. At first, Tara peered at it, thinking it to be ivory. Then she noted the yellowish stains at the base, and the hollowed remains of something else, something—

"May I help you?" the voice, not friendly, spoke English instead of French.

Tara turned. A man stood behind the tiny glass counter, his hands resting on it, but leaving no marks. His black hair was cut short, accenting his hawklike nose and sharp eyes. He wore a perfectly pressed white linen shirt, open at the collar, revealing a tuft of dark hair that disappeared down the button line.

She had no idea what tipped him to her nationality. She was not wearing the American uniform of jeans, a t-shirt, and sneakers. Instead, she wore black pants and a mohair sweater purchased here in Paris. As an indulgence, she had wrapped a silk scarf—the only Hermes she owned—around the sweater's turtleneck.

"Oui," she said in French, a language she had been fluent in since she was three. "I am curious about the relics."

His face did not soften as she had expected it to. Usually French shopkeepers loved to discuss their wares. Perhaps the attitude was different here on the Right Bank, near the Louvre, the Tuileries, and the Seine, one of the greatest tourist areas of Paris.

"I cannot vouch for the True Cross," he said, still speaking to her in English. "They did not give certificates of authenticity at the Crucifixion."

Tara didn't smile because he hadn't meant that as humor. He'd been completely serious. It seemed everyone she met lately had no sense of humor, and she missed it.

She was afraid she was losing hers as well.

She frowned at the man. She did not know him; she was certain of that. She hadn't seen him when she was Abracadabra Incorporated's most successful troubleshooter. Nor had she run into him during her corporate climb. And she was certain he had not come to her new shop, Enchanté.

Instead of answering him, she turned back to the relics, and continued studying the ivory dagger. Its surface was uneven, chipped slightly, and lined. Most ivory was smooth, even after hundreds of years, and it had not turned yellow at the base.

She peered into the hollow end and started. No one had removed a hilt. Instead, there appeared to be organic material inside, dried and molded to a hollow center that went halfway down the ivory itself. Not a dagger then.

A tooth.

Her stomach tightened. The tooth wasn't round enough to be a whale's tooth, nor was it long enough to be an elephant's tusk. The tooth was flat on both sides, and sharp on the edges, coming down to a perfect point at the tip, almost like an arrowhead, only without the groves so often found in anything manmade.

"May I?" she asked in French, her hand hovering over the tooth.

"The sign says not to touch." His tone was as surly as he was, and his English was formal enough to let her know that he didn't practice it much.

"That's why I'm asking," she said, giving up and switching to English. Let him be surly, and let him know he was right. She didn't care now. She wanted to see the tooth.

He left the brick counter. She could see him reflected in the glass shelves. His black pants were as neatly pressed as his linen shirt was. He wore a pair of shiny black boots that clicked on the ancient enamel floor.

He stopped beside her, and brushed her hand away, as if he were afraid she was going to get something noxious on his precious relics. "What is it you want to see?"

"The tooth," she said.

A slight tension seemed to run through his body, then he nodded once. He opened a small cupboard beneath the shelves and removed a single leather glove.

As he slipped it on, Tara realized how quiet the shop had grown. She could no longer hear the constant shush-shush of traffic or the conversations of passing tourists. Instead, all she heard was her own breathing, short and raspy, and the rustle of the shopkeeper's expensive clothing.

He slipped his gloved fingers beneath the tooth, moving gingerly. The tooth hung off both ends of his hand, looking impossibly large as he lifted it away from the light.

"You may not touch," he said. "It is too sharp and you might get the cut."

His voice had lost some of its surliness now that she had responded in her native language, so she did not think to correct his English nor did she give any indication that he had misspoken.

Instead she studied the tooth, itching to touch it, to see if the lines in the surface ran deep or were a result of use, like the chips seemed to be.

"What kind of tooth is it?" she asked.

"A tooth of the dragon," he said.

Even though a part of her had expected that answer, a chill ran down her spine. All of her desire to touch it vanished. She had to resist the urge to clasp her hands behind her back.

"If that's true," she said, "it's a dangerous item to have lying around."

His gaze met hers. Obviously, most tourists did not have that response.

"It guards my treasures as it was meant to," he said, finally reverting to French. "And my signs do warn you not to touch."

Not to touch. Such a simple command for such a complex action. She had never seen a dragon's tooth outside of the Academy, and that tooth had been defanged, so to speak. It had had centuries of white magic practiced

6

over it and in later years, it had been bleached to remove the poisons.

Still, that tooth had throbbed with an energy that she hadn't encountered anywhere else, an energy that could easily become addictive if she wasn't careful.

And the memory of that energy left her struggling to keep her hands clasped in front of her, to play the part of a curious tourist instead of a former employee of Abraca-dabra Inc.

"Are you sure it's authentic?" she asked.

His gaze met hers. He recognized the game she was playing.

"It is not for sale," he said.

They were speaking French and his surliness was gone. In fact, he seemed a little frightened, as if he did not want to think about the liability he held.

"Then why is it on the shelf?" she asked.

"I have told you. To protect my merchandise."

"So you have something even more valuable than a dragon's tooth?"

That would be hard—and rare. Pure dragon's teeth were priceless, as difficult to find as the creatures that they came from. She had never met a dragon. She'd heard that a few still survived, but then she'd also heard that dragons were the comedians of the magical set, which she didn't believe.

A funny dragon couldn't be scary, and a scary dragon couldn't be funny. She knew that much.

She also knew that modified dragon's teeth were somewhat common. In the Middle Ages, wealthy mages drilled holes in the poisonless back teeth, and inserted precious gems. Those teeth could still be found in most of the real magic shops throughout Europe, although they too commanded a hefty price.

"I have items," the shopkeeper said, sotto voce, "if you are certified."

He almost made it sound like he kept pornography in the back. She half expected him to show her a dirty picture.

But she knew what he meant. He wanted to know if she had a magic certification, a convenience certain areas had adopted to make the sale of magical items easier. Shops that required certification from strangers were more common in places with a heavy tourist trade.

She supposed she should not be surprised that she encountered one on the Right Bank.

But she was surprised. Paris had been her home base, more or less, for the decade she ran around the world like an insane person, trying to make sure that all the little magic shops franchised by Abracadabra Inc followed corporate policy. Eventually, she gave up trying to find an apartment—it was difficult for the French to get an apartment in Paris; an oft-traveling American had an even tougher time—and got a permanent suite at the Hotel Intercontinental.

She was staying at that hotel this time. They had missed her, called her by name, told her that they had been quite reluctant to give up her suite.

She hadn't really missed them. She had spent most of her time in that suite asleep on the decadently thick mattress of the queen-sized bed. Asleep or being awakened by yet another urgent phone call.

Initially she had liked the hotel because it was close to La Place de l'Opera and the Vendôme and some of the best shopping in a city that was made for shopping. But in those days, she never had time to go on anything except on an emergency spree when she needed new clothing for yet another country in yet another climate.

So when she came back to Paris, she promised herself that she would spend three whole days shopping, sightseeing, and partaking of the heady nightlife. Then she would get down to business, visiting the dusty shops behind twisty stairwells in Le Marais and the less-traveled areas of the Left Bank as well as the arrondissements where the tourists never went.

A buying trip, she had told her new employee—but she had never said all that she would buy. Yes, things for the shop, but also a few things for her like an extraordinarily expensive pair of shoes that she would probably never wear at home, a skimpy little designer dress that would sit in the back of her closet waiting for a special occasion, and the most perfect scarf she could find—one that cost more than the shoes, one that was made of the finest silk and yet was casual enough to wear in Enchanté every day of the year.

"Mademoiselle," the shopkeeper said, and Tara blinked at him, looking up slowly.

She had been staring at the relic and thinking about her trip. Imagine if something else had been on her mind—the amount of money in her pockets, for example, or the safety of her jewelry in the hotel safe.

She had heard about magics that pulled surface details from the mind. She had never so easily succumbed before.

"You are certified?" he asked, only this time he was speaking English.

And he had called her Mademoiselle, which was accurate. She was thirty-five, and she'd had surprisingly few relationships—certainly none strong enough to turn her into a Madame.

She smiled at the thought. It didn't play in English. The shopkeeper looked at her strangely.

"Yes," she said. "I am certified."

Then she dug into her bag—a terrible Gucci knock-off that she'd brought along precisely because she was going into a touristy area. She had wanted the pickpockets to think she was a poor tourist, not worth their time, rather than a woman whose decade of overwork had left her moderately wealthy.

She showed the shopkeeper the ridiculous piece of parchment that the Society of French Mages had given her gratis for all the work she had done, controlling and destroying the dark arts throughout France. Normally, certification through the Society cost several thousand dollars and included a long (exceedingly dull) course on the history of magic, as well as a test for the most basic skills. She'd been able to skip all of that. First, because it was more than clear she had the skills, secondly because in her position as Chief Troubleshooter for Abracadabra

Inc, she probably knew more magical history than most mages, and thirdly because they wanted her on their side.

Certification lasted a lifetime. They couldn't revoke it.

The shopkeeper's bushy dark eyebrow raised. "Your certification is French."

His voice held surprise. She was getting irritated enough at his attitude that she almost added she had been certified in each country that had joined the program, but she didn't. The French Society had the strictest regulations, the toughest test, and the most prestige.

So far as she knew, she was the only American to have their blessing.

"I wouldn't have thought French certification a problem," she said.

"No, no, it is not," he said. "It is simply—unusual."

She smiled at him. "Then we are both full of surprises."

"Oui." He set the dragon's tooth back on its shelf. The ivory glistened in the light. Then he pressed a button on the side of the counter. "One moment."

She crossed her arms and resisted the urge to tap her toe. She didn't like being this close to the tooth. The longing to touch it had returned. Just one finger along its edge, to see if the ridges were scaly like she remembered…

A poster moved toward her, startling her. Then she realized she was looking at a door as it opened. The door obviously led to the supply room. A delicate woman came out, her black hair cut in a perfect wedge, her makeup—in varying shades of red—dramatic against her pale skin.

She was yelling at the proprietor even before she stepped into the shop—something about interrupting her valuable work.

He snorted. "Watching soap operas is not valuable, except to the television, nor is it work, not even for you."

The woman's eyes narrowed. Her black turtleneck and tight black Capri pants showed off a perfect Cyd Charisse figure.

It wasn't until she turned toward Tara that Tara realized the woman wasn't beautiful at all. Her nose was too big, her eyes too small, but with that alchemy that all French women seemed to know, she had transformed those features into something more than beauty, something arresting.

That aspect of French femininity, or more precisely, Parisian femininity, had always unsettled Tara, and made her feel like the hayseed American no matter how trim her figure or how perfect her clothes.

Perhaps that was how the shopkeeper had recognized her nationality—it was innate, revealed in each movement, each gesture.

"You do not look magical," the woman said with all the spite she had shown the shopkeeper.

Tara shrugged. "That's probably a good thing."

The woman made a dismissive noise and moved to the back of the counter. There she picked up a fistful of postcards and shook them at the man.

"They do not sell if they are not on display," she said as she stomped toward the spinning racks in the front.

The man turned to Tara. His movements were slightly courtly now, as if she were the one he wanted to charm. Perhaps he wanted her to forget the other woman's rudeness.

"The items are in the back," he said, as if the interruption had not happened.

Tara got that vague sense of the pornographic again, as if he were leading her to something unbelievably dirty.

But she also knew that was her innate Americaness coming out. The things American thought were pornographic, the French often called art.

The man looked over his shoulder. "Come with me."

He took a key from the counter, and walked to a gap in the shelves. The gap was covered with a floor-to-ceiling poster of the Eiffel Tower in various stages of completion. All of the images were black and white photographs, clearly taken by the same photographer nearly 120 years before.

He stuck the key into what appeared to be a girder on the side of the half-finished tower. The tumblers clicked audibly, and a door opened.

With his left hand, he flicked on a light, and beckoned Tara to follow him.

Tara walked around the counter and to the door. The air here smelled faintly of vanilla candlewax and Chanel perfume—probably from the woman outside. The light coming from that back room was thin and narrow.

Tara went through the door.

And stopped so suddenly that it felt like a hand had shoved her backwards. The shopkeeper frowned at her from across the space.

"I thought you were certified," he said.

She was. But she also had long-established protections against dark magic. They would not let her go any further.

"How long has this room been here?" she asked.

He shrugged. "As long as the building has, I suppose."

Clearly he had no idea how long that was. But she did. At least a hundred years. This close to the Louvre, probably more like two hundred years.

The room, and its terrible secrets, had been here just as long.

If she squinted, she could see potions foaming in the distance, sending noxious fumes into the air, a thin shade of a former resident working on even more nostrums, and an entire cabinet—built into the wall and invisible to the untrained eye—filled with body parts from someone's former enemies.

Tara shuddered. She couldn't hide her reaction, but she doubted the shopkeeper noticed.

"You did not build this then," she said. "And you are not certified."

He smiled at her. "You are smarter than you seem. I can't go all the way back, not yet. There are spells in place that are older than I am."

She could see through most of them. He had no idea what he had here. "Yet you managed to collect these things."

She was playing dumb, hoping he would talk. Pride. Pride often worked, no matter who the person was, no matter how guarded he seemed.

"I wish I could claim that," he said. "But it is a treasury, that much I know."

And his wife—or whomever that woman was—did not agree.

Tara didn't want to seem too inquisitive. Now her main goal was to leave without disturbing too many of the old spells.

"Did you discover this when you bought the shop?"

"Oh, no," he said. "I've known about it for years. Is there anything you would like to see?"

All the dragon's teeth he had would be a nice start. The box of spell recipes in the very back—something on the edge of it looked like Rasputin's mark. If something of his was here, she wondered if she might find something from Robespierre or even Charlemagne.

And she shivered again.

"Do you have an inventory?" she asked.

The shopkeeper looked at her oddly.

She shrugged, making the movement as Gallic as possible. "I did not get into the French Society by being incautious."

His eyes narrowed, just like his wife's had. He was probably trying to figure out if the American was being naturally rude or if she was trying to tell him that he had been careless, coming into this place without the proper training.

"I have no listing. I suppose I could make one."

"No," she said. "That's all right. I am on a buying trip for my own shop—a little magical place in the Loire Valley.

That shop's been there since the 12th century, and I must call my assistant before I explore too deeply in a treasure trove like this. I didn't expect to find something this untouched on the rue de Rivoli."

"No one does," he said, coming back out. He didn't seem to notice the green cobwebby film that encased him. Tara backed away. When she reached the door, she paused, waiting for him. He stepped out, then stopped to turn the key in the lock.

As he did, she ran her fingers together in a remove and dissolve spell. The web disappeared in a cloud of green smoke.

He saw the smoke. "Did you do that?"

She shook her head, and told him only half a lie. "It came from inside your room."

"The room unsettled you, no?"

"Yes," she said. "I thought I knew all the magical places in this part of Paris."

"I am gathering it was a secret for a long time. Even I did not know for ten years, and I worked here for nearly fifteen years before buying the place."

Now she was getting somewhere. "When did you buy it?"

"Just last year. The previous owner—he—" and again, the shrug "—did not come to work one day. And then the next, and the next, until I finally called the family. They never found him, but he never came back."

Maybe the previous owner was the shade she had seen inside the room.

"Eventually, they had him declared dead or unfit or something like that. Anyway, they received the ability to dispose of his things. His family sold me the shop and its wares at a bargain price."

"And that's when you found the dragon's tooth," she said.

The shopkeeper shook his head. "I had always known of that. Only he had it on a different shelf, closer to this door. I was not to touch it except like I showed you."

Even then, that was dangerous. But she didn't tell him.

"Nor was I supposed to sell it. I suppose I could now, but it seems—I don't know—disrespectful, somehow."

"I would be most interested in it if we can come to a price," she said.

"Let me consult my books," he said. "How long are you in Paris?"

"Only a few days," she said.

"Tomorrow, then," he said. "Come back and we'll see if we can reach an agreement."

2

She escaped the shop, careful not to make a grimace of disgust as she stepped out the door. The wife/girlfriend watched her with undisguised hostility, and Tara made certain to smile at her.

The woman did not smile back.

Then Tara meandered down the sidewalk, pretending to look in the windows of the other shops, when really she was checking her reflection for any other spell that might have been placed on her.

She had suffered two that she knew of: the superficial scan of her mind, started by the dragon's tooth, and the wall of dark magic that her own protections had stopped her from going through. She had no idea how many others lurked in that place, taking unsuspecting innocents by surprise.

Fortunately, the man who owned the shop now had so little magical ability that he couldn't go through that dark wall—not because he wasn't certified, as he believed, but because the darkness didn't want him.

The dark arts, particularly the old and subtle kind practiced in that hidden room, required a certain level of innate ability. Obviously the man didn't have it. Tara doubted his wife did either.

As she stepped past Angélina's, her gaze caught the pastries displayed in the window. She loved this restaurant, often having breakfast here on the days when she had time. She resisted the urge to turn inside now, recognizing the urge for what it was: a need for comfort.

She glanced over her shoulder, but could no longer see the magic shop and the grumpy woman manning the sidewalk displays. So Tara picked up her pace.

Some of the spells in that store could have been repeaters: the scan most likely was, one that triggered whenever anyone stared at the dragon's tooth too long. The spell would happen whether anyone was nearby to receive the information or not. And the scan spell had been powerful to get through her defenses.

Tara shuddered, and nearly ran the last few blocks to the hotel. A row of cabs was parked haphazardly outside the doors, disgorging that day's round of new guests. Tara didn't want to get near any of them.

If the spells she'd been contaminated with rubbed off, then she was sending unfiltered magic throughout Paris. She wondered how many visitors to that shop stared at the tooth, and how many carried that magic throughout the city.

Fewer now that the tooth had been moved to the back of the main room. Quite a few when the previous owner had been around.

The low-ceilinged lobby was filled with tourists, dropping their bags, talking, looking around. The bellmen were scurrying from one set of dropped luggage to another, handing out claim checks so that the luggage would get delivered to the correct room.

Check-in was one of the few times she saw the leisurely French move with any sense of purpose. She always thought that was because they hated the foreign clutter in the lobby, preferring its usual pristine state to the chaos that currently reigned.

Another cluster of people waited in front of the elevators. She avoided them, and headed for the stairs, careful not to touch anything. Fortunately, she was in good shape—her room was on an upper floor. She got there, opened the door with her keycard, stepped inside, and heard the door latch close.

Then she slapped the magic off her as if it were a cluster of nasty spiders. She brushed and recited neutralizing spells, and actually dug into her herb bag for secondary remedies.

Each remedy she tried took another layer of magic off her. That place had been poisonous, and her defenses hadn't caught it.

Either the mage who had set up the spells was extremely powerful, or the magic was really old.

Or, most terrifyingly, both.

She showered, washed her hair with a special shampoo Abracadabra had designed for its troubleshooters, something she hadn't had to use in months (and she hadn't missed it—the stuff smelled like sulfur), and when she got down, she used a spell to gather her clothes, bind them, and stuff them in a laundry bag. The bag would go into a garbage bag she got from the maid, and then they would go off to the one professional cleaner in Paris who could handle magically contaminated items.

She hoped her scarf would survive. She loved that thing, and like most Hermes, it was old enough to be irreplaceable.

When she was dry, dressed, and calmer, she sat on the edge of the bed, and contemplated her options.

If she were still a troubleshooter, she would contact the home office, send the specs about the store, and ask for backup. But she wasn't a troubleshooter any more. Her status with Abracadabra Inc was as an affiliate now, an owner of a magic shop who, if she followed the corporation's rules, would hear from them only through the monthly letter and at dues time.

One of the rules for affiliates was no interference in other businesses. She couldn't even act as a concerned citizen. Instead, she had to go through the baroque reporting procedure, which had only been slightly updated since the baroque era, and the update was not an improvement.

It was a phone number—a phone number connected to a phone tree.

She hated phone trees. She often thought of zapping them out of existence, but that would be an inappropriate use of magic.

Although she had always felt there couldn't be a use more appropriate than zapping the annoyances of the world into oblivion.

Fifteen minutes of answering questions and pushing buttons on her cell phone later, she finally got a person, who rudely told her that there was no magic shop at that address on the rue de Rivoli, and hung up.

Tara stared at her phone for a long moment, and resisted the urge to fry its internal components and send the entire thing to gadget hell. She shrugged mentally, gave up, and dialed a number she was supposed to have forgotten when she quit her troubleshooting job.

She called Quinn.

3

QUINN WAS THE COORDINATOR, a man she had never met, one who sent the troubleshooters to their newest jobs. He had held the position since Abracadabra Inc opened in the 19th century, or so the joke went, although Tara didn't believe it was a joke.

She had never met him. The entire time she'd worked for Abracadabra Inc, she had only communicated with him via e-mail, fax and phone.

For the first time ever, she counted six rings before someone picked up. Quinn, who said gruffly, "This line's now forbidden to you."

"Well, I've come across a serious problem, and the voice at the end of your reporting line wasn't that cooperative. What're you doing, hiring college students these days?"

"Of course not," he said, but the gruffness had left his tone. He knew Tara well enough to know that when she said "serious problem," she wasn't bluffing. "Is there a problem at Enchanté?"

"No," she said. "In fact, business is so good, I decided to splurge and treat myself to a Paris buying trip. I'm calling from the Hotel Intercontinental now."

He didn't chit-chat. "Then what's the issue?"

"I walked into one of those little tourist shops near the Louvre, and found a dragon's tooth."

"Along with a piece of the True Cross, I'm sure."

She could almost imagine him rolling his eyes. Almost, because she wasn't really sure what he looked like.

"As a matter of fact, there was a splinter of wood next to it, and if that's the True Cross, I'll give you a box of La Maison chocolates. But the dragon's tooth is real."

"Real?" That caught his attention, just like she knew it would. She recounted everything that had happened to her in the store as well as her suppositions and her fears.

Then she ended with, "If this is an Abracadabra Inc. store, you need to shut it down. This owner isn't powerful enough to maintain what he has. But I don't remember anything on our listing about a rue de Rivoli store, and this was my territory."

"We don't have anything there," Quinn said, and she could tell from his tone, he was about to end the call and take care of the matter.

"I want to help your troubleshooter," Tara said.

"It's not your job any more," Quinn said.

"I know." She wiped a hand over her face. The skin was smooth—no green cobwebs covering it. She would be checking that for days. "But almost no one has the skill to deal with this kind of magic, especially alone. It might take months to get two of your best operatives together, right?"

Quinn sighed. "It feels like you never left."

That wasn't a yes or a no, so she continued. "I think this is too much of a threat to leave on its own while your people gather, particularly with that undetectable magic being spread around. Pull your best troubleshooter from whatever she's doing—"

"He," Quinn said.

"—and I'll help him."

"You haven't done the updated training work," Quinn said, which was required of all troubleshooters.

"And I won't, since you're not hiring me," Tara said. "You're bringing me out of retirement for one last shot."

"I worry that you're not current with the spells," Quinn said.

"Neither is the mage running the place. He's pretty clueless. We should be able to neutralize the shop until you decide what to do with it."

"Why are you arguing so hard to be involved?" Quinn asked. "I thought you had burned out of this work."

Good question. It was Tara's turn to sigh. She had learned over the years that the only way to deal with Quinn was to tell him the truth.

"This place scares me," she said.

"You're never scared," Quinn said.

"I used to be," she said, "when I started."

"And then you learned how powerful you are," Quinn said.

"Which is something I still know." Tara's voice was soft. "I certainly wouldn't go after this place alone, not even if my training was up-to-date."

He whistled softly. She moved her ear away from the phone until the sound ended.

She had finally impressed him.

"I must warn you," he said softly, "that our best, while excellent, is not quite as good as you."

She nodded, but didn't say anything. She wasn't sure if Quinn was flattering her now that she was on the team or if he actually meant it, and she didn't care. She wanted to get rid of this place, finish her shopping (that as-yet unknown pair of shoes called to her), and go home.

She missed home.

Then she smiled. It was actually nice to have one.

"His name is Alistair Grint. I'll have him contact you."

"Grint," she muttered. Had she heard of him? The name sounded vaguely familiar. "You know I have an appointment to go back there tomorrow."

"If Grint hasn't reached you by then, keep the appointment, but don't do anything," Quinn said. "He's on some remote island in the Pacific. Getting him to France is going to take some time."

Since the corporation didn't allow its employees to travel via magic, claiming such travel sapped them of the magical reserves and drew attention to their strangeness, it would take at least a full day.

"In the meantime," Quinn said, "I'll contact a few others. They're all on major cases, but they should be able to free themselves in a week or so. You'll have backup. I just don't know when."

"Thanks, Quinn."

"Don't do anything stupid."

"Have I ever?" she asked.

"Not until today."

She couldn't tell if he was serious or teasing her. Probably serious. Who would jump back into the fray after declaring herself free of all that? Especially on a project like this one?

"I'll let you know when we have this thing under control."

"Do that," Quinn said. "I'll be waiting."

4

QUINN WASN'T THE ONLY ONE who waited. Tara had her cell set on its loudest ringtone. She avoided crowded places, getting herself a baguette at a boulangerie, some camembert and ham from a nearby grocer's, and making do with a picnic supper in the Tuileries.

Making do was a little dramatic. The Tuileries were amazing at this time of year—the trees in full leaf, the flowers blooming. Children rode on the carousel, and half a dozen American tourists jogged along the paths, looking trim and important.

The French meandered, staring at the various statues or leaning against them while talking on the phone. The French were trim as well, but Tara blamed that on the prevalence of smoking.

She did get some shopping in, splurging on an Hermés bag to go with her favorite scarf, but left every store she was in the moment the voices of the other patrons grew too loud.

She no longer felt like she was on vacation. She felt like a woman who had managed to sneak an afternoon off work. And that brought back the raggedy panic of those last few years at Abracadabra Inc. Not panic that she was unable to do her job, or panic caused by fear of the black magics she saw, but panic that came from exhaustion, burn-out, and a sense of being trapped.

The sooner she was done with this project, the better.

And that made her wish for Grint's call all the more.

So of course the call never came.

5

Tara dressed differently for her second visit to the shop. She wore a white blouse she had purchased the night before at one of the lesser fashion stores in the Galeries Lafayette, and a pair of all purpose black pants. Her shoes were reliable black walkers, and she carried that same Gucci knock-off purse she had during the first visit, only this time it had bags of herbs inside and half a dozen protection spells around its outside.

She figured she might be searched for the prevalence of white magic, but she knew her bag wouldn't be.

It didn't help that she was irritated. Grint could have called from anywhere, telling her when to expect him. But no. The man was inconsiderate enough to believe that the work would wait until he got there.

He probably didn't care that she had an appointment at the store. It would have been nice to coordinate something with him in advance—maybe even a time to make another appointment—but of course, he wasn't even that considerate.

Quinn knew that she liked planning and schedules and everything done to the letter, and he would have communicated that to Grint. Grint had clearly chosen to ignore it, which irritated her even more.

Her walk down the rue de Rivoli was reluctant. She pretended at window-shopping, but her heart wasn't in it. She was thinking, as she had been all morning, about whether or not she really wanted to buy that dragon's tooth. If she paid for it and removed it from the shop, would she really make the area safer? Or would she be making things worse by altering the magic that so clearly flowed from that secret room?

She had no real way of knowing, not without some study.

She had looked at her old databases, which she still kept on her handheld. Nothing Abracadabra Inc showed that a magic shop had ever stood on that site.

But that didn't mean anything. The darkest magics could be hidden for generations, only to reappear with a viciousness if their flows were obstructed.

Caution told her to leave the tooth there. Which meant she was going to have to be a difficult negotiator, accepting no price except something so outrageously cheap that the owner would have to refuse.

The postcards rack and a stand of tiny Eiffel towers stood outside the door to the shop. That woman was nowhere to be seen. No tourists stopped either. They walked by, looking at the same postcards or perusing the t-shirts in another store along the way.

Tara paused as she reached the stand of Eiffel towers. Someone was inside the store. She could hear a booming male voice, followed by the owner's sullen one. She peered in.

The owner stood behind his counter, arms crossed. He wasn't quite leaning on the display behind him, but it seemed like he was. He was watching the man on the other side of the counter with a mixture of reserve and curiosity.

That man was taller than the owner, with blond-brown hair that brushed his collar. He wore cowboy boots, tight jeans, and a leather jacket that seemed too warm for the weather.

His attitude—and that booming voice—limited him to two groups: German or American. As she stepped inside, she realized she was hearing French spoken with a Texas twang—something as bad as hearing The Marriage of Figaro sung off-key.

American then.

Both men glanced at her. The owner looked relieved. "I have an appointment," he said in English.

Tara recognized the game as the same one the owner had played with her the day before.

"Well, Tara can help us," the customer said in French.

She had to hold herself rigid so that she didn't start in surprise. This was Alistair Grint?

She'd expected a prissy British guy in a bespoke suit, maybe even carrying an umbrella. She hadn't expected a cowboy with a broad Texas twang.

He was continuing in that twang: "Her store, Enchanté, in the Loire Valley, has been part of the corporation since—when, Tar?"

She hated being called Tar. She hated being surprised. And she hated losing control of her own investigation.

"It predates me," she said with a smile, coming all the way inside. She spoke French as well. "I had no idea you were in Paris, Al."

She couldn't call someone from Texas Alistair. She just couldn't.

"Doll," he said—and that word was in English, although the rest of what he had to say wasn't—"I live for this city, you know that. How come you didn't look me up when you got here? There's some new places in the 18th Arrondissement that you gotta see."

In spite of herself, she blushed. Many of the businesses there still provoked an American good-girl reaction out of her. The bisexual theaters, the gay lounge acts, the naked revues shocked her, even though she had seen all sorts of bizarre things in the magical community.

"Lookie there," Grint said to the owner, and this was in English too, "I got her to blush. Works every time."

Her blush deepened, and for a moment, she felt like she had as a new hire at Abracadabra Inc.

"Doll, tell him about our company. Seems he's never heard of us."

She hated the "our company" part. She hadn't planned on identifying herself at all. She was going to let Grint be the bad cop. Maybe she still would.

"I'm not sure how much you'd call it mine," she said, still speaking French. "I'm like you, Monsieur—? I never did catch your name."

"du Vigneaud," the owner said, his surly tone even worse.

"Monsieur du Vigneaud," Tara said. "I'm Tara Miller."

He nodded, clearly not pleased at the introduction.

Grint said, "Mademoiselle Miller has owned her shop for, what?, a year?"

"Two," she said, her tone as sullen as du Vigneaud's.

"And I'm sure she's quite happy with us."

Her gaze met du Vigneaud. He didn't look happy. She wasn't either, at least at the moment. She wasn't even sure how to play along.

"I barely notice the corporation," she said. "It's really more of an affiliation. I can get supplies cheaper than anywhere else, and if I have magical troubles, I can send for one of their experts. Fortunately, I didn't have to suffer a sales pitch though—"

And with that she glared at Grint.

"—since the previous owner had already joined the organization. It was a condition of sale that I stay in." She made herself sound reluctant.

Grint's blue eyes narrowed just a little, as if in annoyance. He had one of those angular American faces—the kind that suggested too many years outdoors, not enough vegetables, and a lot of hard living.

"Honestly," she added, "you probably don't need the corporation. You're primarily a tourist shop with some magical wares. I'm mostly a specialty magic shop. I get almost all my supplies through them, but you have many other suppliers. I can't see any great benefit."

"Except the protection of more mages than you know what to do with," said Grint, who had switched completely to English now. "This close to the Louvre, and all that nasty Paris history, God knows what could be around here. You could stumble into a pile of leftover spells and not even know what hit you."

"I have an appointment," du Vigneaud said. He hadn't said anything else since Tara arrived.

"I assume that appointment's with you?" Grint asked.

"We made it yesterday."

"Can it wait? I'd love to buy you lunch, catch up on old times."

"Perhaps dinner," Tara said. "Perhaps tomorrow. Call my hotel. I'm at the usual place."

"The usual place." He nodded as if he knew where that was, then smiled winsomely at du Vigneaud. "She's quite the catch, you know. Every time she comes to Paris, I try to convince her to stay, but she won't. You know how women are."

"Most certainly I do," du Vigneaud said. "It is quite the coincidence that she is here and you are here. Odd that you would meet in a place with magical items."

He didn't say a magic shop. Tara found that interesting.

"Well, we initially met in one. I'm the one who told her that Enchanté was up for sale. I was just gossiping, I had no idea she was looking for a place of her own, or I wouldn't've said anything. I really didn't want her in the far reaches of the country, if you know what I mean."

"One could always follow her. Salesmen seem—what is the expression?—footless?"

"Footloose," Grint said. "Yeah, and that's the problem. There's more for us footloose types in Paris than in those tiny villages out there in wine country."

"I do not live in a tiny village and we do not call the Loire valley wine country," Tara said stiffly. She had decided. She hated Alistair Grint. "Listen, I'll come back. It's clear that you and Monsieur du Vigneaud have much to discuss."

"No!" du Vigneaud sounded panicked. "My appointment is with you, Mademoiselle. He just came in, saw my shelf, and started telling me about this corporation of his. You do not think it worth my time?"

"Magic isn't your focus," Tara said. "Or at least it doesn't seem that way."

"But with my—" And he nodded toward that door. It would have looked to Grint like he had nodded at the dragon's tooth. "—you do not think it would help with sales or perhaps my own training?"

"Your training's another matter," Tara said, but Grint spoke over her.

"We offer continuing ed classes all the time, and not all of them here. You and the wife—you're married, right?"

du Vigneaud nodded, his expression tight.

"Well, you and the wife could go to New York or Saigon or Sydney all in the name of continuing ed. Sometimes, if your skill level requires it, you can get a grant that'll pay your way. A few of these places take newer members for free, just to get them acquainted. Imagine a trip to the far reaches of the—"

"I'm leaving," Tara said again, feeling irritated. She almost had him convinced to join, not that it mattered. She had no idea why Grint was pursuing this path.

"No!" du Vigneaud said. "Please, don't leave."

He turned to Grint. "Leave some literature. I will think of your proposition."

Grint sighed. He took some brochures that had Abracadabra Inc. written across them in red out of his leather jacket and set them on the desk. Then he turned to Tara.

"The usual hotel?" he asked with a leer.

"The usual hotel." She kept her voice cool. She decided it didn't matter if she showed how annoyed she was. Her mood matched du Vigneaud's.

Maybe she could use that to build commeraderie.

"I'll call you later, then," Grint said, saluting her with a single finger to the forehead. She hadn't seen that move in years—it was very American, and very out of place here.

Then he sauntered out of the shop, whistling as if nothing had gone wrong.

She shook her head.

"I'm sorry about that," she said to du Vigneaud.

"Why should you apologize?" he replied in French, which startled her. She had reverted to her Midwestern roots, apologizing as a way of opening a conversation. She hadn't done that in a very long time.

"I feel embarrassed that I even know him."

"You know him well, it seems."

"I knew him well," she lied. "Once. Suffice to say that I'm not at the usual hotel."

It took du Vigneaud a moment to understand what she meant, but once he did, he grinned. "You are sly, Mademoiselle."

"I'm tired of pushy American men," she said.

"I can understand that." du Vigneaud shoved the brochures aside. "May we talk about the tooth then?"

She smiled, even though she didn't really want to do this negotiation now. She really wanted to chase after Grint, berate him for ruining the moment and not even setting up a plan.

Instead, she said, "I've been doing some research on pricing. Even then, I'm not quite done."

"Research can take forever," du Vigneaud said.

"It can, can't it?" She had to pull herself together. She needed just a momentary diversion. "May I see the tooth again?"

He walked over to the shelf, removed the tooth as he had done the day before, and draped it over his hand. It seemed even larger than she remembered.

She took her jeweler's loupe from her purse, mostly as a pretense, yet another stall. The tooth didn't intrigue her as much today. She didn't feel her eye drawn to it, nor did she feel that sense of getting lost in her own thoughts.

Perhaps the spells on her purse were working. Or maybe something in those brochures blocked the magic. She wouldn't put it past Grint.

She leaned over the tooth, put the loupe in place, and studied the tooth. It lacked the ridges that held the poison, and the ivory itself seemed too smooth.

"May I?" she asked, and without waiting for du Vigneaud's permission, she ran a finger on the tooth.

No frisson of magic, no sense of panic. The tooth didn't even feel odd. Instead it seemed like—

"Plastic," she said.

"What?" du Vigneaud asked.

"This is plastic," she said. "The one from yesterday, it was real. But this is not."

He peered at the tooth as if he had never seen it before. "It's…"

Then he ran his finger over it, closed his fist on it, and glanced at the shelf, as if he expected the real tooth to materialize.

"It's not real," he muttered, as if he hadn't noticed before.

"Nice scam," she said. "But if you wanted me to pay you for the tooth, you shouldn't have let me touch it."

He shot her a wild-eyed look. "We were going to negotiate. I wasn't even sure I was going to sell it."

"So take it out of that back room, and let me see it," she said. "I'm glad you decided it was too dangerous to leave out front, but really, my magic is strong enough that I can tell a fake tooth from a real one with only a cursory glance. You shouldn't have underestimated—"

"Mademoiselle," he said with panic in his voice. "I did not take my tooth to the back room. It was here, where it always is, when I closed the shop last night. The only time someone touched it…."

And again, his voice trailed off.

Tara felt her back tense. "Yes? The only time you touched it?"

"Was to show it to your friend." du Vigneaud looked at her as if Grint was all her fault. And actually, his presence was her fault. Kinda. She would never have brought him in here like this. She had had a completely different scheme in mind.

She would have told him that if he had bothered to consult her.

Which, of course, he hadn't.

"You didn't notice the tooth was different when you showed it to me just now," she said. "How could you have noticed if it was different when you showed it to Al?"

"I didn't," du Vigneaud said. "But he was studying it like you had yesterday for some time. I left him there, praying he would leave, and when he did not, that was when I finally talked to him."

Only the French. Tara resisted the urge to shake her head. Customers had to be worthy of a proprietor's time here, and if they weren't, they were welcome to leave. It seemed worse in Paris than anywhere else, but she had noticed it in Nantes and a few other cities as well.

"Did he touch it?" she asked.

"I don't think so," du Vigneaud said. "But how am I to know?"

"A dragon's tooth is a powerful thing to steal," she said. "He would have had trouble conversing with us the way that he had. Did you have other customers today?"

"None that were near the tooth."

"Were you here the entire time?"

His eyes narrowed. "My wife, she opened the shop."

Tara shrugged, making sure the movement was smooth and Gallic. "Then perhaps she took it to the back and put the fake tooth out here. Why don't you see if you can track it down, and I'll be back tomorrow. We can have the discussion then."

"What of your friend?" du Vigneaud asked.

"What about him?" Tara asked.

"What if he took it?"

Tara sighed. He probably had, the bastard. "I can't imagine it. I've been assured that the employees of Abracadabra Inc are honest people."

"Assured?" du Vigneaud asked.

"It is uncomfortable to give an organization so much control over your livelihood," she said, lying again. She really liked the corporation. It had been good to her. "That's why I wasn't very enthusiastic when he tried to sell you on it. I can't see any benefit for you."

"What if he's not honest?" du Vigneaud asked.

"I still can't imagine him stealing something like that tooth," she said, and this time she wasn't lying. He would have had to use a powerful spell to overcome the tooth's magic.

"He asked you to dinner. Perhaps you could call him? Perhaps you could find out for me?"

Tara frowned. He was trusting her. Had that been Grint's plan? Did Grint even have a plan?

"I'll find out," she said, making herself shiver. "Even though that means dinner with him."

"Thank you, Mademoiselle."

"But," Tara said, "I won't take it from him. I'll just tell you what I find out, if I find out anything. All right?"

"Yes, fine," du Vigneaud said. "I will see you tomorrow, no?"

"Tomorrow, then," she said, and walked out of the shop. As she turned toward her hotel, she noticed du Vigneaud through the window. He was staring at the fake tooth as if his heart had been broken.

She had made it to Angélina's when someone grabbed her arm. Without turning around, she elbowed her assailant in the stomach, heard a satisfying "oof!" as he let go of her, and kept walking. She clutched her purse tightly to her chest, wondering what else could go wrong on this day.

Footsteps sounded behind her, determined footsteps, not the footsteps of some window-shopper. Heavy breathing, and a little bit of moaning.

She braced herself for another elbow defense, but this time as the assailant grabbed her arm, he said, "It's Grint, you idiot."

Only the words came out rather breathy. She had gotten him good. Amazing that he could follow her—usually someone who got her elbow in his stomach was down for the count, even if she didn't use magic (which she hadn't, this time).

"I'm the idiot?" she said, shaking him off. "You're the one who decided to go the case alone. You're the one who handled the entire thing like an ugly American, a move that guaranteed du Vigneaud would be angry at you. You're the one—"

"Tara, please." He still sounded winded.

She eyed him sideways. "I found this place. I reported it, and frankly, I could have handled it with a lesser trouble-shooter, but they insisted on their best, who decided not to call me."

She stopped, forcing him to bang into her. She turned, pushed him back so that they were at arm's length, and added, "I used to be the best troubleshooter at Abracadabra Inc. You were working there at the time, so don't play ignorant. Just because I retired doesn't mean I've lost my skills. You could have at least had the courtesy to call me and tell me you had arrived. When you hadn't, I assumed you weren't there. Then I run into you and have to play along like a rookie, watching you ruin the entire thing—"

"I didn't ruin it," he said

"You stole—"

People looked at them. She lowered her voice, almost to a whisper.

"You stole the dragon's tooth. Did you think he wouldn't notice?"

"I hoped he would," Grint said.

"Do you know how dangerous that is, carrying a dragon's tooth around with you?"

"Would you put it in your purse then?" he asked with a grin. "It's amazingly well shielded. What did you do? Shrink down Fort Knox and hide it in there?"

Her face heated. She hated blushing, and he'd gotten her to do it twice now.

"We have no plan, and he thinks you're a thief. Which you are. Maybe when he gets over the shock of losing his most prized possession, he'll realize that you and I know each other and that we might both be involved."

"So?" Grint asked. "We got the tooth. Troubleshooting done. You've got enough spells on that purse that we could send it to Headquarters with the tooth inside and no one would be the wiser."

"You are dumber than you look!" she snapped. "The tooth was never the issue. Didn't you talk to Quinn?"

"He said the shop'd been there forever, and the tooth twigged you to the power hidden at the site. So? If you had played along better, maybe du Vigneaud would have joined Abracadabra Inc, and we wouldn't have had any issues at all. Now we're just going to have to keep an eye on the place—"

"Were you jet-lagged when you talked to Quinn or were you just drunk?" she asked.

Grint frowned. "Why?"

"Because there's an entire other level, filled with things so powerful that I can't even get inside. My wardings won't let me. And you just notified whatever's down there that someone is onto it."

"Huh?"

"The tooth, you idiot. Who do you think is controlling it? Not du Vigneaud. He didn't even realize you put a fake one there until I pointed it out."

"You pointed it out? Why? I used an excellent replica that would have bought us days if not weeks."

"Bought us days, not weeks, for what?" she asked.

Grint shrugged. Apparently he hadn't thought that far ahead. "Getting him to join our little club."

Tara rolled her eyes, pivoted, and continued walking.

"Tara, wait!"

But she didn't stop. She was done with this. Their best troubleshooter had come in, shot at trouble, and missed. It was no longer her problem. She wasn't even going back tomorrow to finish her "negotiation" with du Vigneaud.

"Tara!"

She hurried, staying ahead of Grint, and as she entered the Hotel Intercontinental, she murmured to the doorman, "That man is harassing me."

The doorman nodded, and put a solid arm out to stop Grint from following her inside.

She made her way to the elevator before turning to see what was going on. Grint was arguing with the valets and doorman, waving at her as if she wanted to save him.

She turned her back on him. Idiot. Fool. What the hell had he been trying to prove, anyway? How brilliant he was? Because if that was the case, he had failed.

6

THE PHONE IN HER ROOM rang incessantly. She finally un-plugged the thing. Grint could call all he wanted, but she wasn't going to talk with him.

She had already called Quinn and complained, saying their boy had screwed things up, and she was done. The shop on the rue de Rivoli was their problem; she wasn't going to work with a certified nutcase.

Quinn's response had surprised her. He had chuckled. "There's a reason Alistair works alone," he had said, and then had thanked her and hung up.

Tara fell back on her bed, feeling at loose ends, angry and concerned all at the same time. She knew the shop wasn't her problem, but she worried about it anyway. A person didn't simply discard ten years of training in an afternoon. And the magnitude of the problem bothered her as well—all that magic being distributed over one of the most cosmopolitan cities in the world. Probably being distributed all over Europe as well.

The fact that they'd sent someone as incompetent as Grint—and called him their best—also bothered her. She knew the other troubleshooters weren't on her scale, but she had never realized how sub-par they actually were.

Which meant that the problem in that shop might remain.

She rolled over, balled her fist, and closed her eyes. She should go to a shoe store, head to a clothing store, or buy herself some chocolate. Maybe the concierge could tell her what was at the Opera tonight. Something—anything—to keep her out of that back room.

But nothing would.

She knew it, and Quinn probably knew it. In fact, he probably counted on it.

Knowing the old bastard, he had probably sent Grint just to make her this angry, so that she would do her very best work one more time.

What was it about her that made her so worried about stray magic? Whatever it was, it had made her a troubleshooter with a hundred percent clearance rate, and it had nearly destroyed her life.

Now that she found peace, she was going to give it all up for a basement magic lab that had probably existed when Paris was a walled Roman city.

She sat up. If she got caught, she would have no back-up, no help, no one to turn to. This would be the most dangerous job she had ever done—and dammit, she was looking forward to every minute of it.

7

She dressed all in black, hiding her hair beneath a very ugly black ski cap that she still carried everywhere, even though she thought she would have no legitimate reason to sneak into legitimate businesses any more. She wrapped her workbelt around her waist. The belt carried all her herbs and her dispel potion. She had thrown it into her suitcase at the last minute, wondering why she was bringing it along.

Maybe she had had a premonition.

She smiled. She never used to believe in premonitions. Maybe she had been giving herself a subconscious message—one that she hadn't realized she needed.

She didn't want to think about that. She left her cell phone on the table beside her bed—if things went wrong, calling for help wouldn't work—and then she tucked fifty euros in various pockets scattered around her skin-tight pants.

Cat burglars always had to be prepared.

Now for the tough part. She couldn't teleport directly from her hotel room—anyone with minor magical skill could follow her magic trail and figure out where she originated—so she had to leave the hotel. She could double-teleport—go to one location, and then to the next, which still left a magical trail, albeit one that was harder to trace—or she could walk out of the hotel, looking like Grace Kelly in To Catch a Thief. Only without the patrician features or Cary Grant lurking at the other end.

Tara sighed. The hotel was used to her. If someone noticed something out of the ordinary, they'd attribute it to her strange personality or her occasional American lapses.

She slipped her keycard into the only pocket on her shirt, and then left the room.

No one gave her a second glance on the elevator, or as she walked through the lobby, or as she stepped into the street. Apparently black was considered stylish in Paris, in any combination. She crossed the street, and headed down the stairs at the entrance to the Tuileries.

Mages used the gardens all the time. If she did a reveal spell, she'd find a dozen fresh magical trails, all of them leading to different parts of the city. That was the reason Abracadabra Inc had put her up in the Hotel Intercontinental in the first place—easy access to the Tuileries and the Louvre. The magic trails died off the closer one got to the more modern marvels of Parisian life: the Arc de Triomphe and the Eiffel Tower. Magic's most important Paris enclaves were nearest the Seine—the Louvre, the Tuileries, and on the Left Bank, the Sorbonne. (There were a few trails that led past Notre Dame, but no one discussed them, out of respect.)

She stopped near a statue of a horse, put her hand on its stone flank, and waited until no one was within eyesight. Then she recited a very old, very slow-moving transport spell.

As usual, it took a moment before the magic swirled around her. This spell was less of a disappear-from-one-location, reappear-in-another kind of spell, and more of a fade-to-black, find-yourself-somewhere-new kind of spell.

If anyone did watch at all, they'd see a woman grow more and more transparent as she stood near the stone horse, until they wondered if she had ever been there at all.

Eventually the cool stone ceased to touch her hand, and she was in that dark limbo which used to unnerve her. As an early mage, she wondered if this was what death felt like. Now she found the silence, the darkness, and the warmth comforting, rather like falling into a deep sleep in the perfect bed.

Moments later, she felt something dig into her hip. She was gaining solidity near the stupid counter of the stupid shop, and she didn't dare move. Moving during this spell could have tragic consequences. A few practitioners died each year using it, but even more got the wrong body part attached to the wrong part of the body.

She hissed in her breath, noting a sulfur smell that had not followed her from the Tuileries, and wishing the transport would hurry up. When the spell finally ended, she banged, literally, against the counter, as if she had stumbled into it, just like she knew she would.

She cursed, rubbed her sore hip, and took note of her surroundings.

The mundane world security was as poor as she had expected. The cameras above her were for show: they weren't working at all. The magical security was present, but low-key—at least the stuff du Vigneaud had put into place. It was rudimentary but solid, more than enough to catch the average non-magical thief.

Which she wasn't.

She neutralized his work in a matter of seconds. But that sulfur smell remained, unnerving her. Did someone want her to notice it? And trace it? Or was that a sign of the older magical security system, the one that Grint had probably damaged when he removed the tooth?

She didn't have any answers for that.

Still, she went back to that shelf with the relics, just to make sure du Vigneaud hadn't replaced the fake tooth with another real one. He hadn't. The piece of the True Cross looked like the splinter that it was, and the other relics had even less splendor to them. Apparently du Vigneaud added a glamour every day to his shelves, just to make the merchandise that much more attractive.

Poor guy. He had no idea that his little tricks wasted what little magical potential he had. And they probably played right into the hands of whomever or whatever controlled that room behind the Eiffel Tower poster.

Tara squared her shoulders and faced it. The poster glowed redly. She turned, to see if any lights from the street caused that red glow, but she couldn't see any.

The glow was coming from the hidden room itself.

"Creepy, huh?"

Tara jumped, so startled that she had to stifle a yelp. No one ever caught her off-guard, and yet someone had.

She turned toward the voice. Grint was leaning on the counter, right about the place where she had banged her hip. He grinned at her, and held up the real tooth.

"It started to glow about five minutes ago," he said. "Just like that little red space back there. Then what happens? I see my pretty little partner staring at the shelves in that goofy magic shop she'd been yelling at me about."

She wasn't sure what to correct first, the fact that she wasn't his partner, she wasn't little, or that she wasn't paranoid. Then she realized how defensive she was feeling, and how off balance he kept her, and she wanted to turn him into a toad, something she hadn't done to an annoying male since she was twelve.

"What're you doing here?" she whispered.

"Getting your back," he said. "Isn't that what I'm supposed to do? Or am I supposed to lead? Or are we really a team? I can't remember. I'm jet-lagged, you know."

She glared at him.

"You shouldn't have brought that here." She nodded toward the tooth. "It's the center for all the exterior magic in this place."

"Oh, you think?" And his snide smile faded as his sarcasm grew. "You're acting like I had a choice."

Her breath caught. "What do you mean?"

"I mean, I saw you, and then got teleported right here, against orders."

She wasn't sure if against orders meant that he shouldn't teleport (which was a major rule) or that he shouldn't help her any more than necessary.

She decided not to ask.

"Since you have the key to the kingdom," she said looking at the strangely pulsating tooth, "you get to go first."

His face paled noticeably, even in the weird red light. "You're kidding. Through that poster? What do you think I look like, a French version of Alice?"

The image that provoked in her mind was so ludicrous that she had to swallow a laugh.

"Yep," she said. "Let's go through the looking glass, Mademoiselle."

"That's not funny," he said, gave her one more glare for good measure, then felt around the poster for the door latch.

Tara crossed her arms. If he had simply asked her where the latch was, she'd tell him, having gone through that door before. But of course, he was annoyingly independent, and right at the point when she was going to show him, the door clicked open.

Revealing a smoky, hazy room beyond, filled with that pulsating red light.

The sulfur smell grew.

"I don't like this," Grint said.

"That's not what it looked like before," she said, more to herself than to him.

He glared at her for the third time. "You've been in there?"

"If you had bothered to consult with me before you barged in here today, and if you had tried to talk to me like an equal before you stole the tooth, and if you hadn't accosted me on the rue de Rivoli this afternoon, you might have learned that there's an entire room back there, maybe even a sub-basement or an old Roman construction, something that goes very deep. It's filled with all sorts of scary things, most of which my warding spells wouldn't have let me near. But since you didn't, and since Quinn seemed to have neglected to tell you, then you get to go in that space first."

"Huh?" Grint asked.

She grinned. "You get to go first."

"Fine." He shoved the tooth in his shirt pocket—upside down so that the pointed end stuck out over the fabric—and went inside. The smoke swallowed him, swirling as if he'd never been.

Then it dissipated.

The room was there, but there was no Grint, and there was no tooth.

"Wonderful," Tara said, this time to herself since there was no one else around. "That's just great."

Now she had to not only figure out what was going on here, she also had to rescue Grint.

That was why she had always worked alone.

She hated rescuing people, particularly men. Men were always too embarrassed to say thank you.

Since the pulsing light and the swirling smoke had swallowed him up so quickly, she hesitated near the door. She wanted to find the spells that he had triggered.

There were the usual warnings, wardings, and weak wizardings, nothing serious enough that a troubleshooter for Abracadabra Inc could get caught in. She extended her hand and did another reveal spell, looking for magical trails or some subtle indications of warding spells. But she didn't find any—and that unnerved her.

Until she realized what had happened.

Grint had the dragon's tooth, which coordinated the exterior magic in this building. The building had been broken into, and the tooth did its job. In its nonsentient, magical way, it brought what it considered the perpetrator to the entrance of the magical chamber, where he got sucked into the magical punishment area—wherever and whatever that was.

She shuddered. Early in her training, she'd been subjected to a few of those spells, just so that she could figure out how to extract herself from them. She hoped Grint had had the same kind of training.

The sulfur smell was gone. The potion bottles in the very back of the secret room no longer bubbled like they had the first time she'd seen them, and she couldn't see the shade of a former patron. Maybe the shade had gone to take care of Grint.

She shuddered again.

Then she squared her shoulders, sighed heavily, and removed several of her own warding spells. This was the part that frightened her the most. She knew she'd have to remove some protections she'd had for years just to go back into that area. She would have to keep her wits about her at all times—the worst thing about older magical areas was that some of the spells around them warped thoughts, and she didn't know any counter spells for that.

The thought-warping spells had been banned for centuries, and the counterspells lost—if there ever had been counterspells.

A tinge of excitement sent butterflies through her stomach, and she tamped them down. The place she got hooked—the place she was the weakest—was on historical spells: discovering what had been lost. If she was honest with herself, she wanted to see those spell recipes in the very back. They'd intrigued her from the first.

And since she wasn't working for Abracadabra Inc, she could keep them if she wanted to.

She shook that thought away, wishing she could blame it on a warp and knowing that she couldn't. She'd had similar thoughts in Venice when she'd found a secret passage that actually went under the waters of the canal and led to an old magic potion bottle disposal site. She'd wanted to dig through those bottles as well, keep the secrets for herself, and not tell anyone what she'd found.

But she'd overcome that. Just like she would overcome this. So long as she cleared her mind before she went in.

She spread her arms, and did not use a magical spell to clear her mind. She'd tried that on half a dozen occasions, only to have stronger magics sniff out the spell and reverse it.

Nope. She'd found the best way to clear her mind had nothing to do with magic, and everything to do with the physical world around her. She took several deep breaths, used some calming techniques she'd learned in a long-ago yoga class, and then counted to fifty. Her heart rate slowed, the butterflies left her stomach, and some tension she hadn't even realized she'd had eased out of her shoulders.

She felt stronger, more able, and ready to face what was ahead. She stepped through the poster-covered door into the barely lit room beyond—

—and nearly gasped at its size. The room seemed narrow from the outside, but inside it went back away from the front door for what seemed like blocks. (Which wasn't possible: yes, there were large buildings here, but they ended, and other buildings started on the other side of the block, and then there were other streets like the Rue St.-Honoré and her favorite chocolate store, and traffic and— she sighed. It wasn't an illusion, but it was something like an illusion. She'd have to figure that out too.)

To her left and right, the room extended as well, going through the back of the building as if it were a corridor or a long river that served as a divider between sections.

When she turned to examine this, the blocks-like illusion which ran in front of her, seemed narrow again, as if whatever it was that went left to right bisected the longer area in front of her.

Confusion started to swirl in her brain, and she couldn't allow that. Confusion let other magics in. If the confusion remained, she would have to do more calming techniques, which she really didn't want to do.

Instead, she took another step forward. The images shivered and shook, the potion bottles bounced on their shelves, and a cat walked across a dusty table. Tara smiled. Finally she understood. She was going through waves of spells, designed by various owners of this space, all of whom had their own theories about what an intruder should see.

Maybe Grint's initial ploy hadn't been bad after all. If du Vigneaud had joined Abracadabra Inc, the shop would technically have belonged to the corporation and a lot of these security spells would have been neutralized. Instead, she was going to have to go through a long magical procedure, one that could take most of the night, to make them go away.

She raised her hands to start the spell, when she realized she could try something else. She backed out of the room, closed the door, and did a simpler spell, one that made her look and seem—for all intents and purposes— like du Vigneaud's wife. The illusion would only last a few minutes, but that was all she needed to get to the heart of that room.

The "intruder" had already been caught by the most recent security spell. Grint had helped her in that way. The magic would have no idea that she wasn't who she seemed.

She pulled the door open. Then she went inside again. The room—the real room—was old and smelled of damp. The Seine or Paris's famous sewers had backed up in here one too many times. She resisted the urge to sneeze, never knowing what might tip the magic to her disguise.

The room was as small as it had initially looked. It was narrow and dark, with cobwebs looping off the stone walls and ceilings. This then, was how du Vigneaud had gotten covered with cobwebs on their first visit in, and probably what had stopped Tara in her tracks.

She shivered, knowing that this time, with her protections gone, she was probably getting covered with the same greenish webby stuff that had covered him the first time.

She stepped forward. Normally, she would do a small spell for illumination, but she didn't dare. There had to be a system in place, one that triggered when someone who had the rights to enter this room did.

And sure enough, her disguise worked well enough to activate the light spell. Lights flared as she past the first column of stone. The lights, magical as they were, imitated the original creator's time period—so instead of electricity or even gaslight, she was faced with a candle floating before her, and torches hanging off the stone walls.

Water dripped past the torches, adding to the chill. The room veered slightly to the left, revealing a staircase that went down, down, down with no end in sight.

If she were still with Abracadabra Inc., she would go back outside and double-check her backup. But she wasn't, and the corporation had actually failed her this time.

So she crossed her fingers and hoped that whatever she found down here—whatever she learned—would be worth it.

The steps were sunken in the middle as if time and many feet had worn them away. The water dribbled down the side, a constant trickle that should have worn away even more of the stone decades ago.

Some of her deepest protections had awakened now, but she had muted their automatic powers, so all she heard were the occasional warning voices in her mind. She paid attention: each warning indicated a particularly nasty spell, and there seemed to be one ever five steps or so.

She counted the steps, but lost track after 180. She had no idea how deep underground she was going, but she knew there was some distance to travel. A lot of this city was underground, and much of it had been walled off over the centuries. It shouldn't have surprised her that some magical being had taken part of Underground Paris as his very own.

Finally, the steps leveled off. The air was fetid down here, the mildew and mold stenches even stronger. A corridor disappeared into the distance, with no torches lit.

She wondered if that was another illusion, one the woman she was still pretending to be fell for.

Tara didn't dare challenge it, not wearing this guise, and she didn't dare change the guise this deep into the dark magics of this place. So she turned to the right, which was the only direction in which the torches were lit. She followed them only a few meters before reaching one last door.

This one was oak with metal reinforcements. The wood had grayed, and the metal had rusted around all of the very old bolts that held it in place.

As she pushed the door open, it creaked. A man, younger than she was, looked up from his place behind a solid mahogany table. He had dark eyes, long dark hair pulled back into a queue, and a thin, narrow mouth.

"You're not Suzette," he said in modern French.

She hadn't expected to be caught so easily, nor had she expected to hear someone down here speak the modern version of the language.

"No, I'm not," she said, but she kept her disguise, knowing that sometimes the magic could be tricked even when the mage wasn't. The last thing she wanted was to change back to her normal form down here, only to have the dark magic form around her, trapping her in place.

"What're you doing here?" the man asked.

"I could ask you the same thing," she said. "You're running a dark arts shop. That's against all the covenants of the modern era."

It was a weak argument, but the only one she had since the shop wasn't a member of Abracadabra Inc. All members of the corporation swore off the dark arts the moment they joined. She had had to enforce that little provision more times than she cared to think about.

Only once before had she faced a dark arts practitioner without the backing of the corporation's bylaws. And that particular little meeting hadn't gone well.

"Do I know you?" he asked, and this time, she was convinced he was trying to get her to reveal herself so that the magic could take her. Which might mean that she had an unexpected advantage.

If he was truly worried about her (and the repetition suggested he was), then he should have used his own powers to stop her. He wasn't. Or he was unwilling to. Which meant he either had no dark powers or he had no access to them.

Or, conversely, he could simply be lazy, not willing to use his powers until he absolutely had to.

She hoped against lazy. "I doubt it. I work for Abracadabra Incorporated."

Or at least she had on previous jobs. She had to mentally qualify her statement because sometimes lies were dark magic magnets.

"For what?" he asked.

"Abracadabra Incorporated? You might recognize it by its old name—Alchemists United For the Common Good," she said that last in English, and added the acronym. "You know, AUCG." Which she pronounced Oooo-guck.

"AUGC?" He frowned. "You've changed your name?"

Bingo. She had a time frame for this guy. Abracadabra Incorporated had gone through a number of incarnations over the years, all as legal business entities. The first was in the 16th century, and put together under England's Guild laws. Then it had been the Pure Alchemists' Guild—pure as in white magic, not as in sexual purity. AUGC was the 19th century version of the organization.

"We changed the name to Abracadabra Incorporated, yes," she said, returning to French.

He stayed in that language as well. "Mon Dieu, I thought you people were wedded to your Common Good moniker. I always hated that."

I bet you did, she thought but didn't say. She didn't need to argue with him about morality and magic which, if his training was pre-Victorian, was where the conversation was headed.

"Obviously so did many other members," she said. "I take it you're not one."

"Do I look like a do-gooder to you?"

Actually he did, with that smooth face, the warmth in his eyes, and the sparkle about him. But the sparkle was what clued her. No one looked that friendly, especially not someone who'd been working in the dark arts for the better part of two centuries.

"You look like a man at work," she said. "I found your security system. Quite elaborate. But you shouldn't have based it on that tooth. It can be moved, you know."

"Not without killing its mover," he said.

"You haven't kept up with modern spell protections, have you?" she asked. "Most anyone with a bit of training can hold a dragon's tooth. Your assistant did so all the time."

"Suzette?" he asked again.

"Her husband," Tara said.

"The idiot," the mage said. "She was supposed to warn him to stay away from it."

"Obviously that worked," Tara said, then wondered if the mage before her would get the sarcasm. He pursed his lips at her tone, and she realized she needn't have worried.

The room around him was curiously blank. Tara found it hard to focus on the walls, the floor, the ceiling. And she couldn't really see any objects in there besides the man and the table. Another illusion spell? Or was he yet another protection, buried deep in the magical system.

"Suzette's new, isn't she?" Tara asked.

"More or less," he said, looking down at the paper before him (paper, when there hadn't been any a moment ago). He was feigning disinterest, but he also might have been showing her that there were other things in the room.

He was another protection, one designed for the shop's owners. How many generations of mages had he tricked?

"How new?" Tara asked.

He shrugged. "Why do you care?"

"Because," she said, "I want to know what you're hiding here."

He looked up. "Nothing. As you can see."

That was it. The room was filled with nothing. Not so subtle after all.

She decided to go for broke—or whatever suitable cliché she could think of. She wrapped her own magic tight around her disguise and went into the room.

Suddenly the pulsating red light was back, along with the sulfur smell. She half-expected a demon to appear before her, but none did. She was grateful: she hated demons. Most of them were simply mages with puffed up egos.

The man had disappeared. In fact, the entire room had disappeared. Instead, she found a gaping hole that opened even deeper into Paris's underground.

"Hey, Tar?" Grint's voice floated up from the deep hole. "You here yet?"

He was trying to sound cool, but he actually sounded panicked. Terrified. About-to-lose-everything-including-his-mind crazy.

She decided not to answer him—not because she was being mean, but because she didn't want to tip off whatever was there, holding him.

Instead, she pulled her tool belt so that it was as tight as it could be, plugged her nose, and cannonballed into the billowing smoke.

8

AN HOUR LATER, maybe more, she surfaced. She had no other word for it; it wasn't like her brain was being probed or she had lost consciousness. No, it was more like it was off, the way it went off under anesthesia—no dreams, no thoughts, no nothing. One minute there and the next minute not-there. She had no memory of falling, yet she knew she had fallen for a long time, and was still falling.

She hit some kind of surface, bounced, and realized that she wasn't in France any more. Or any France she recognized. The surface beneath her hands, her feet, her butt, was a clayish mud. The air still smelled of sulfur, but the naturally occurring kind, the kind she'd seen around hot springs.

The pulsating red light was now above her and looked a lot more like a short-circuiting neon light than some kind of glowing pulsating evil. The walls arched over her, and even though the ceiling was open, in other sections, it had already closed.

She had landed in a cave.

Of course.

She smiled and shook her head. Then she stood up, brushed as much of the clay off herself as she could, and called out, "Hello!"

When all that echoed back to her was her own voice, she added greetings in every modern language she knew. Then she went for the medieval versions of the same things. It wasn't until she tried Latin that she got an answer.

In English.

"All right, already. If you're going to shout all day, I'm going to end up with a headache."

The voice was twenty times louder than hers had been. It literally shook the walls.

"Come visit, come on. You're so damned determined, I suppose we may as well be face-to-face. But I have to tell you if there's armor or a sword, tell me now. I like my knight roasted."

Tara's smile grew. A dragon. A dragon that, for some reason, had a shop on the rue de Rivoli. A dragon that, for an even more inexplicable reason, was trying to sell one of its own teeth.

Tara walked forward, past very old and yellowed skulls, some suitably charred bits of metal, and one rather unnerving mummified hand. After a few minutes, she reached the section of the cave where the ceiling was still intact, and she braced herself for some old claustrophobia, but it didn't hit. Apparently her brain registered the size of the cave—more suitably called a cavern—and deemed it large enough to keep her blood pressure level.

A slight incline, a forced corner, and she was in an even larger cavern, one with some kind of natural light that came through the ceiling. The ceiling material—she couldn't quite call it rock—glowed whitely, like opaque skylights. And in the very back of the cavern the dragon huddled.

It looked rather small and a little plain. Even though the creature was twenty to fifty times Tara's size (she never was good at comparisons), it still seemed unprepossessing.

"All in black," the dragon said, lifting its snout to talk rather like an alligator in a cartoon. "How disappointing. I thought fashion in the 21st century would give up on the basic black."

Tara moved to a rock near the dragon's right eye. Even though she'd never encountered a dragon, she did remember her lessons about them: 1) Never stand directly in front of one; 2) be polite; and 3) always look them in the eye.

That last was specific. Eye, not eyes. Eye was polite. Eyes was impossible unless you violated Rule Number One, which often led to accidental charring and a particularly hideous death.

"I dressed like this because I was entering your shop after hours," Tara said.

"Cat burglar." The dragon sighed. "Which is an odd phrase, considering that you don't look like a cat. Then I guess the black makes sense. I had just hoped, you know, for a green season, or perhaps the return of pink."

The return of pink? Was the dragon being serious or were the rumors true? Was the dragon trying to be funny?

The idea actually chilled Tara. She finally understood how something could be amusing and dangerous at the same time.

"You brought me down here to discuss fashion?" Tara asked.

"I didn't bring you down here. You jumped, insane human that you are. I actually had to hit the air currents so that you wouldn't splat against my lovely floor. I hate it when humans splat. Everything gets mushed, and the bones usually shatter, taking all the fun out of breaking them for marrow."

The threats sounded like the dragon didn't have his (her?) heart into them. They seemed almost rote.

"I just wanted to see what was down here," Tara said. "I work for Abracadabra Inc—"

"Yes, I heard the entire tedious conversation, and realized that you were going to get past every fail safe every half assed mage I hired over the centuries tried to assemble. So I resigned myself to having a visitor. I haven't had a female one in nearly two centuries. There is only so much information you can pick up from the Style Network."

Tara frowned. "You get television down here?"

"A rather elaborate and at times magical theft from the roving satellite systems. I much prefer the variety of American television, but I can get everything from Al Jazeera—which isn't nearly as biased as your American newscasters make it out to be, to Telemundo. The Mexicans have the best soap operas, by the way, but no fashion sense."

Tara had a distinct feeling of unreality, even stronger than it had been when she'd been dealing with illusions.

"You spend your time down here watching television?"

"And movies," the dragon said. "And I still read when I get the chance, but it's hard. Books are very fragile things. I'm beginning to prefer the audio downloads."

"A computer too?"

"A new one every week. I still can't manage a keyboard for long." The dragon rolled its eye. The eye looked very reptilian—gray-green-brown, with no visible lid and no lashes, and a lot of cold intelligence.

Tara shook her own head slightly. "I can't believe I'm having this conversation."

The dragon's eye slitted, making this side of its face, at least, look menacing. "You're humoring me."

Tara sighed. She hadn't expected to be caught, but this creature was so much older than she was. Longevity always bred its own wisdom.

"You're right, I am humoring you," Tara said. "I've never encountered a real dragon before. I'd been expecting—I don't know—the shade of a mage who couldn't let go or a power reservoir designed by Charlemagne or something."

"Romantic." The dragon curled its paws under its chin. "That's your problem. Charlemagne. As if he would ever need a place like this."

"You knew him?" Tara asked.

"Of him." The dragon's eye widened. "As I said, I don't get out much. And you people have the lifespan of fruit flies, comparatively speaking."

"Then why set up the decoy shop? Why not lose the entrance to this cave altogether?"

"eBay, child."

"Hmmm?" Whatever Tara had expected, it hadn't been that.

"I get shipments like everyone else. Every treasure ever invented gets auctioned at one time or another." The dragon's scaly lips pulled back in something that might have looked like a smile—at least from the front. But Tara wasn't going around front to check.

"You order things from eBay?" Tara couldn't quite wrap her mind around it. "How do you pay?"

The dragon sighed. "Really. A thousand years of hoarding does give one enough wealth to open a Pay Pal account."

Tara frowned.

The dragon let out a disgusted moan. Smoke curled from its nostrils, and a small lick of fire escaped between its teeth. It put its claw over its mouth.

"Sorry," it said, "but I do that when I'm annoyed."

Tara's stomach clenched. "I didn't mean to annoy you."

"I know, dear." The dragon burped, and the stink of sulfur grew. "It's just that I thought you were more intel-

ligent than you really are. Here's how it works. I get a minion. What's her name this time? Suzette? And appear to
her in human form. She has never been down here, thank
the gods. I hand her a gold piece or a ruby or some such
nonsense, tell her to sell it, let her keep ten percent for
herself, and give the rest of the funds to me. That keeps
my little Pay Pal account active for some time."

"How do you know she's not cheating you?"

More smoke curled. "I can get satellite reception
down here. How hard do you think it is to do a little magical spying of my own? That's how I lost the last minion.
He decided to keep ninety percent for himself, and give
me ten."

The dragon sighed again.

"I should have known, too. He was always a problem,
even when we were dealing in real commodities. And he
was stringy."

"Stringy?"

"I actually had to send the new minion for some special floss. His tough skin got caught in my teeth." The
dragon raised one lip and pointed with a claw. "See?"

Tara didn't want to look. "You still have some skin
there?"

"No, silly. But I do have a puncture in my gum that
has yet to heal. See?"

Tara squared her shoulders and peered into the re-
cesses of the dragon's mouth without getting close. Sure
enough, there was an indentation that looked inflamed.

"Surely you can magic that away," Tara said.

"Do I look like a dentist to you?" the dragon snapped. "Some things are harder than they look."

For someone who could create a hole in the earth? Monitor what was happening on a Paris street from whatever this distance was? Get satellite and computer technology without getting caught?

Tara wanted to ask those questions, but didn't. Instead, she asked another.

"So what about the tooth?"

The dragon closed its mouth. "You belong to that whiny jerk?"

"You have Grint?" Tara asked.

"If that's what he's called. He looks stringy too."

"It's the times," Tara said. "Thin is in."

The dragon made a note of disgust. "Is he yours?"

"Never met him before yesterday," Tara said, wondering if she was dooming him, and if she was, how she could save him. "He's been annoying me too."

"These creatures don't seem to think about how their bossiness and their complaining plays. They act tough, and then when they're trapped, they blubber like a baby. It's not attractive." The dragon's pupil moved oddly, as if it were focusing on Tara in a whole new way. "You're not blubbering."

"I'm not trapped," Tara said. Then her stomach clenched tighter. "Am I?"

That weird smile raised the side of the dragon's lip. "That depends. Are you going to tell Abracadabra Inc. about me?"

Tara had to force herself to keep breathing. She promised herself she wouldn't lie to this creature—it seemed to sense lies. "They need to know what this well of magic is."

"If we concoct some kind of story that allows me to have my minion and my connection to the center of human commerce—"

"You think Paris is the center of human commerce?" Tara asked, unable to stop herself.

"No," the dragon snapped. "Of course not. But it's only five hours from New York, and I can force the minion to go there if I have to. Besides, New York is an island. I loathe water."

"You've already investigated moving there."

That eye movement again, like a camera lens focusing, focusing. "I did, about fifty years ago. Seems like yesterday. I didn't like the bedrock, the silt, or the smell. None of the buildings are old enough and the culture is still too brash for me."

"In other words, you couldn't find a good location for your shop."

"Actually," the dragon said, "call me old-fashioned, but it still feels like I'm heading to the provinces. I prefer a city with history. My first minion was a Gaul, you know. I liked him. Not whiny or bossy."

Reminded of Grint, Tara realized a thread had been left dangling. "You never told me about that tooth. Why would you sacrifice a tooth, even for all the protection it buys?"

"You're an inquisitive one, aren't you?" the dragon said. It moved back slightly, and what had looked like bulges on its back unfolded and then folded again. Wings.

The dragon turned so that it was looking at Tara straight on. Her heart started to pound, but she didn't want to move, at least not right away. She didn't want the creature to realize how very scared she was.

"The tooth is my ex-husband's. It was the only part of him worth saving."

In spite of herself, Tara grinned. "Ex-husband. Dragons have divorce?"

"Good heavens, we live forever. Imagine our society if we didn't have divorce."

"But you got his tooth. Is he dead?"

"Just defanged, honey," the dragon said and chuckled. More flame crept out, licking dangerously close to Tara's feet. Tara scrambled to the side of the dragon's head.

"You're using your ex-husband's tooth to protect your shop, control your minions, and fund your eBay addiction?" Tara asked.

"I don't control the minions," the dragon said with a huff. "I buy them off."

Then the dragon tilted her head sideways.

"Say," the dragon said, "can you be bought off?"

"Of course not," Tara said, truly offended this time. How many dark arts practitioners had tried bribe her? How many had offered her powers they thought she couldn't refuse?

More than she cared to count.

"Really?" the dragon said. "What about the stringy fellow?"

"I'm sure he can be bought off," Tara said with disgust.

The dragon chuckled again. "You really don't like him."

The dragon picked at her teeth with her claw. Then she said, "What I meant was, could saving him work as a bribe?"

Tara finally understood. The dragon wanted something from her.

Tara moved slightly out of the line of fire and sat on a nearby rock. "What do you want?"

"I need a new minion," the dragon said. "These people are too dumb and I'm really unhappy with the level of talent I've seen in the past few generations. I'd like someone with great power to work with me, not for me. You have great power."

Tara felt cold, even though the air here was hot and clammy. "I'm also sworn against the dark arts."

The dragon exhaled a stream of fire. It scorched the earth next to Tara but didn't touch her although the heat seared her skin.

"You humans always assume we dragons are practitioners of the dark arts. We have never gone dark. We just don't like being stabbed in the eye with swords and having our teeth plucked out for magical gain." Each word emerged with a tiny lick of flame. The dragon really was annoyed.

"Tara? Is that you?" Grint's voice was shaking. It sounded very small as if he were far away.

"What are you doing to him?" Tara asked.

"Nothing," the dragon said a little too innocently. "Except making him hold the tooth."

Tara's chill increased. "You realize the magical vibration could kill him."

"It can do that," the dragon said. "It can also tenderize the stringy ones."

"Tara!"

"All right," Tara said. "Let him go and I'll talk with you."

"About partnering up?"

"As long as you promise not to eat me," Tara said, adding, "I've always heard how dragons keep their promises."

The dragon's eye twinkled.

"Liar," she said, then tilted her head back.

Grint appeared next to Tara, his bare feet on the scorched rocks. He screeched and jumped aside. The tooth clattered between them.

Tara felt the tooth's power, even from that distance.

"The woman has freed you," the dragon said. "But before I send you back to your world, I will bind you. You cannot speak of me. You cannot think of me, and you can never come here again."

Then she flicked her tail, and Grint disappeared—without saying thank you, of course.

Tara's stomach jumped. Now she was alone with the dragon, and she wasn't sure she wanted to be.

"If we were to partner, what do I have to do?" Tara asked, when she was sure her voice wouldn't shake.

"Not much. Make sure my internet works. Help with the occasional cable connection. Get my packages down here in a timely manner. And keep quiet about what I'm doing."

Tara wouldn't tell anyone about the dragon. She didn't dare. She would lose Enchanté. A bargain with another magical creature was against Abracadabra's rules.

"That's all?" Tara asked. "I don't have to bring you food? I don't have to help you locate treasure?"

"Child, I've been stuffing myself these last few years. Don't you know anything about dragons? I only have to eat once every half century or so."

Like a snake. The food had to work its way through the system.

The idea that Grint could have been that struck Tara as gross. A long Texas stick, stringy, working its way through the dragon's gullet.

Tara bit her lower lip and forced herself to focus. "What happens if I chose not to be your minion?"

"Partner, child. I prefer partner."

"Partner, then."

The dragon smiled—if that's what that teeth-baring really was. "If I were younger, I'd threaten to kill you or remove your magic or send you back in time or something. But I'm not. And I like you. I like how you manipulated both of those men."

Tara waited.

"You can walk away," the dragon said. "You'll never be able to come to this part of the rue de Rivoli again."

"This isn't the rue de Rivoli," Tara said. "I don't know where we are, but we're not in Paris any more."

The dragon chuckled. "See? Too smart for your own good. The point is, you can walk away with your life, your magic, and your memories intact."

"What do I gain if I help you?"

"Protection for that little store of yours," the dragon said. "You do realize that your precious corporation is going to shut it down?"

A shiver ran down Tara's back. "They won't. I'm a franchise owner."

The dragon snorted. "You're so American. And so are they. That's the problem. Stores older than a century are starting to frighten them. Seems the magic has been around too long to be contained."

Tara frowned. "How come you know this and I don't?"

"You're not corporate any more, darling," the dragon said. "I did some digging when your friend Grint came here. And I have nothing but time. Nothing but time, internet files, and vast curiosity. They'll compensate you, of course. But the store goes."

Tara wondered if that was true. She wondered if she was being manipulated by the dragon.

Then she thought of Quint and the way he had treated her, not letting her solve the dragon's tooth problem, even after ten years of exemplary service. Of Grint, and the way he had looked at her, as if she didn't matter at all.

And of that anonymous woman on the phone at the Abracadabra Affiliates help line, the woman who had snapped at her and hung up.

Tara had been around corporations long enough to recognize the signs of cutbacks. She just hadn't been paying attention. She'd focused on her own store for too long.

"What if I don't want the protection?" Tara asked.

The dragon's wings opened, then closed. It was the dragon equivalent of a shrug. "Then we can come up with something else. The point is, darling, that I need a new partner."

"Minion," Tara said.

"Partner," the dragon said, "and you need a friend. Not to mention some style tips. What do you say?"

Tara frowned. "May I think about it?"

"Be my guest," the dragon said. "I have all the time in the world."

It took Tara a moment to realize that the dragon wasn't just using a turn of phrase. "Much as I'd love to be your guest," she said, "I'd prefer some time in my hotel room. Some time to research things for myself."

"Time to figure out if I'm compromising you?" the dragon asked.

"That too," Tara said.

The dragon nodded. "You can leave any time you want. However, I do sincerely hope that you come back."

Tara actually believed that. She wondered if the depth of the belief came from her own intuition or some kind of dragonish manipulation.

She didn't wait to find out. Instead, she headed to the first cavern. But before she left the dragon's lair, she stopped.

"When I come back," she said, "what should I call you?"

The dragon blinked at her.

"You know my name," Tara said. "You heard me give it to Monsieur du Vigneaud. If you want a fair consideration, give me yours."

The dragon studied her for a long time. Then she said, "Frieda."

It felt right. It felt natural. Like true names did.

Tara thanked her, then returned to the spot in the first cavern, the spot she had landed on. She waved a hand in a transport.

She didn't go through the darkness or the sulfur or anything like what she had gone through to enter.

Instead, she simply ended up near the statue in the Tuileries. She slapped herself, dusting off the magical residue, and slowly worked herself toward the Hotel Intercontinental.

While she was there, looking up the P&Ls for Abracadabra Incorporated, she had a realization.

The dragon's name had been real. True names had power. In the wrong hands, a true name could be used to control, to bind, even to kill.

The dragon had made herself vulnerable.

Tara's heart pounded.

The offer was for real.

9

She shouldn't have accepted. That's what the experts at Abracadabra Incorporated would have told her.

But the dragon was right: Abracadabra Inc. was an American-held corporation, and much as it valued research, it didn't always understand history.

Dragons and humans had partnered since time immemorial, to the benefit of them both.

Only most people believed all the dragons were gone.

Tara looked through her documentation on dragons and realized a lot of dragons were gone, but a few famous ones remained.

Including a canny female with an eye for silk skirts and amazing rubies. A female believed to answer to the name Frieda.

That detail was the clincher. Along with the internal memo Tara had found when she hacked into Abracadabra's corporate network, the memo that suggested a compensation rate of no more than one million euros compensation for each store closed. The million would go to stores that did 100K in euros per year.

Stores that did less than 20K would get 250K compensation. Her store hadn't even done that well; she wouldn't even get a full return on her investment.

Ten years of faithful service. Ten years of four hours sleep per night, of more stress than a human could tolerate, of skipped meals and intercontinental flights. Ten years of fighting dark arts practitioners, putting her life on the line, and what would she get?

Nothing.

She would lose her store, her dream, and she wouldn't even recover her savings.

That, more than anything, made her take Frieda's bargain.

The first thing Tara did was cancel her affiliation with Abracadabra Inc, paying a 5K Euro fee and suffering through more threats than she wanted to think about.

Then she and Frieda moved the opening to the cavern to Tara's store, warding it, and guarding it with the ex-husband's tooth (although deep underground, where no innocents could stumble on the wayward magic).

So far, the deal was paying off. Within a year, Abracadabra Inc divested itself of 90 stores all across Europe. The cutbacks sent awful ripples through the magical world, and made Abracadabra's share price plummet.

Not that it mattered to Tara. She had a new routine. She got six packages from eBay providers every day, a new computer system that she had to install in the cavern every week, and an upgrade of the dragon's television/DVR set-up every year.

And that was all—except for the occasional pink dress, and lifetime subscription to the French Vogue.

She read it so that she and Frieda had something to talk about. But she didn't take advice from the magazine. And she kept wearing her basic black.

She also stayed thin—or as Frieda would say, stringy and unappetizing.

Because it was one thing to believe a dragon's promises. It was another to rely on them.

About the Author

Award-winning, bestselling writer Kristine Kathryn Rusch has published books under many names and in many genres. Her fantasy novels about the Fey have been published all over the world, and were recently released in the United States as audiobooks by Audible.com.

She has won the World Fantasy Award and is the former editor of *The Magazine of Fantasy & Science Fiction* magazine. She also writes fantasy novels under the name Kristine Grayson.

For more information about her writing, go to kristinekathrynrusch.com.

Also by
Kristine Kathryn Rusch